THE PANCAKE CHAMP

JOANNA NADIN

ILLUSTRATED BY ANA GÓMEZ

BLOOMSBURY EDUCATION

LONDON   OXFORD   NEW YORK   NEW DELHI   SYDNEY

BLOOMSBURY EDUCATION
Bloomsbury Publishing Plc
50 Bedford Square, London, WC1B 3DP, UK
29 Earlsfort Terrace, Dublin 2, Ireland

BLOOMSBURY, BLOOMSBURY EDUCATION and the Diana logo
are trademarks of Bloomsbury Publishing Plc

First published in Great Britain in 2022 by Bloomsbury Publishing Plc

A catalogue record for this book is available from the British Library

ISBN: PB: 978-1-4729-9449-3; ePDF: 978-1-4729-9451-6; ePub: 978-1-4729-9450-9;
Enhanced ePub: 978-1-8019-9036-3

2 4 6 8 10 9 7 5 3 1

Text design by Sarah Malley

Printed and bound in China by Leo Paper Products, Heshan, Guangdong

To find out more about our authors and books visit www.bloomsbury.com
and sign up for our newsletters

Chapter One

Manjit was new at school and he hadn't made a friend yet.

In class he sat next to Daisy, but she only wanted to play with Priya.

At lunch he sat with Luca, but Luca mostly talked to Shay.

At break he kicked a football against the wall and wished he was back at his old school.

Until, one wet Wednesday, Manjit found himself drawing a dragon with Leon.

Leon was different to him. He was taller. His hair was curlier. And he was good at video games.

But the boys became the best of friends. They made up jokes. They swapped dinosaur cards.

And, at break, they kicked the football to each other.

Chapter Two

One day, Leon asked Manjit to come round to his house after school.

"How about tomorrow?" Leon asked.

"We can walk home together and my dad says you can stay for tea!"

But Manjit had a panic. He hadn't been round to anyone's house for tea before, and there was a lot to worry about.

"What if they have a scary dog?"
he thought to himself. "What if Leon's
dad's a dragon? What if I lose at video
games and Leon laughs at me?"

But, worst of all, Manjit worried about what they'd eat. What if it was peas? Manjit hated peas. What if it was soup? Manjit hated soup more than he hated peas.

Or, what if it was pancakes? Manjit really hated his mum's pancakes. They were too thick, and too sticky, and only came in lemon flavour.

And Manjit hated lemon more than soup and peas put together.

"I'll have to ask my mum," he said to Leon. "She'll probably say no."

But Manjit's mum didn't say no.
She said, "Why don't you take
your football round there with you?
And if you don't like the tea, just
say you're not hungry."

Manjit was still a bit scared. But he was brave as well. "Okay," he said. "I'll go."

Chapter Three

Manjit's tummy jumped as they waited
for Leon's dad in the playground. But
when he arrived, smiling, he didn't
seem like a dragon at all.

And there were three cats instead of a dog, and nothing was scary – until they played hide and seek and made each other jump.

And there was no time for video games after that, or even football.

But there was time for tea. Manjit's tummy started swirling again.

What if it was soup? Or peas?
Or, worst of all –
   "Pancakes all right for you boys?"
Leon's dad grinned.
   "My favourite!" cried Leon.

Manjit gulped. "I'm... not that hungry," he said.

"I understand," said Leon's dad. "But you might change your mind when you see my pancakes!"

"I bet you will," said Leon.
"He's the pancake champ!"
Leon's dad laughed. "Now
watch and learn."

Chapter Four

Manjit watched as Leon helped
his dad whisk the mixture
until it was just right.

Then he had a go.

Manjit watched as Leon helped his dad pour the batter into the pan, and listened as it sizzled.

Then he had a go.

And Manjit watched as Leon helped his dad flip the pancakes into the air.

Then he had a go.

For a moment he thought his pancake might stick to the ceiling, but then it plopped back down into the pan, thin and crispy, just how he liked things.

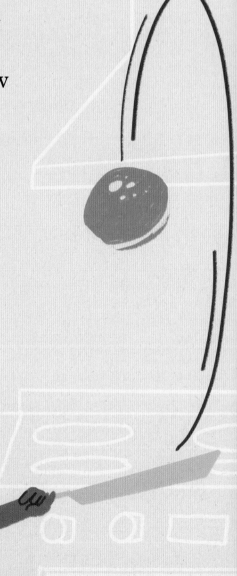

"Bet you're feeling peckish now," said Leon's dad.

Manjit nodded. He had to admit he was. Only –

"So, what do you fancy on top?" asked Leon. "There's anything you want."

Manjit frowned. "What do you mean? Don't they just come in lemon flavour?" Leon's dad laughed. "Not in this house!"

"How about chocolate spread?" said Leon. "Or chopped up strawberries?"

Manjit's mouth dropped.

"Or jam," said Leon. "Or even cheese."
Strawberries? Jam? Cheese? Chocolate?
Manjit LOVED all of those.

"I'll have that!" he said.

"Which one?" asked Leon's dad.

"Oh no," said Manjit. "I meant all of them, please."

Leon grinned. "Me too!" he cried. Leon's dad laughed. "Go on then," he said. "But don't blame me if it tastes weird."

Chapter Five

It did taste a bit weird. But good too.

And so did the apple and coconut ones.

And so did the sweetcorn and
hot sauce ones.

Not even the cats would eat the
ketchup and cucumber kind, though.

"Same time next week?" asked Leon's dad.

Manjit smiled. "Can we have pancakes again?"

"Whenever you like!" said Leon's dad.

And they did.

And do you know what? The boys are still best friends, and still eating weird pancakes today.